# HAL THE PIRATE

Written by June Crebbin

Illustrated by Polly Dunbar

WALKER BOOKS
AND SUBSIDIARIES
LONDON · BOSTON · SYDNEY · AUCKL

## 5 May 1718: Seaside, Devon

Yo ho ho! I started pirate school today! I'm on a huge ship called the "Dragon". Captain Blackbeard shouts so much he keeps making me jump.

We sail tonight - I'm so excited. I'm going to write everything in this diary so I'll always remember my first pirate voyage.

6 May: somewhere out at sea

We set sail at 22.00 hours (that's pirate for ten o'clock), heading west... I think. I never know my west from my east. I had to help let out the topsails. I leant too far back...

Hang on, Hal!

The sea is very wet - and very cold.

Shiver my fingers! Shiver my toes!

Shiver my knees and bum-psy daisy!

## 7 May

Very early this morning I was tipped out of my hammock and ordered to scrub the decks.

Show a leg!

The "Dragon" was rolling and heaving.
Suddenly my stomach heaved too.
I had to dash to the side...

I was so sick, I thought I'd never stop.
I leant too far over the rail...

Captain Blackbeard ROARED at me.

Then he SMILED and said as I liked
the sea so much I could test the plank.

**Later**

I'm sick to the skin of being wet.
At first, testing the plank was fun.
I had to jump up and down. The crew
shouted, "Keep going! Keep going!"

But, at the end, the plank got very
wobbly and bounced me off into the
deep blue sea - again.
Captain Blackbeard ROARED with
laughter.

## 8 May

Today was much better. I had to help Greasy Joe in the galley (that's pirate for kitchen). We made Squiddy Stew.

# SQUIDDY STEW

1. Take twenty or thirty squid.
2. Chop into chunks.
3. Add cabbage, herring, onions and anything pickled.
4. Pour in lots of salt, pepper, mustard and any sauce you have handy.
5. Boil for hours.
6. Serve with gallons of rum.

The best thing was using
a cutlass to chop up the squid.
Great fun! Though it would keep

wriggling about. I can see why
Greasy Joe has two fingers missing.

## 9 May

Not a good night. Everyone was up being sick. I wasn't to know that the red sauce I put in to flavour the stew was Greasy Joe's hair dye!

## 13 May

I've been locked in the bilges of the ship (that's pirate for way below decks) for three days. It's stinking down here. Filthy water swills about, and rats run everywhere!

## 14 May

Things are looking up! I've been let out! It's wonderful to breathe fresh air again.

# 15 June: Windy Straits

We've been sailing for days and days. Today I was put in charge of charts!

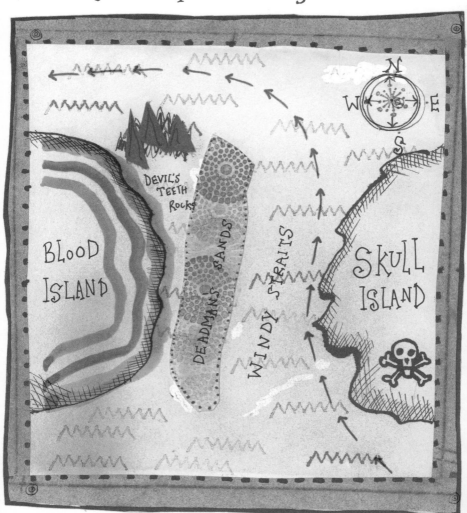

First I plotted the course.
Then I took over the wheel. I held it
steady, though the wind was blowing
like billy-o. I had to keep well to the
east to avoid Deadman's Sands.

Easy-peasy, bright and breezy! I was so happy, I kept bursting into song!

A pirate's life for me,
A-sailing on the sea,
Yo ho the billy-o,
A pirate's life for me!

So hold the wheel steady,
There's food in my belly,
There's rum in my veins,
I don't care if it rains...

A pirate's life for me,
A-sailing on the sea,
Yo ho the billy-o,
A pirate's life for me!

# 16 June: Blood Island

I've been marooned - left here on Blood Island alone. I steered the "Dragon" onto Deadman's Sands by mistake and it got stuck. Captain Blackbeard ROARED at me,

"You don't know your west from your east!"
I watched the "Dragon" all day.
Towards evening it floated off on the tide.
I've never felt so lonely.

You don't know your west from your east!

## 24 June: a cave
When I explored the island I found a tiny bubbling stream. But I haven't eaten for three days.

Fish swim rings round me ...

lizards play hide and seek ...

and monkeys scream
with laughter when I
try to catch them.

25 June: the other side of Blood Island
I saw the "Dragon" today! On the beach!
Captain Blackbeard must have sailed
back to the island for repairs.

Some of the crew were scraping the "Dragon's" bottom - to get rid of sea creatures that like to cling there!

**27 June: the "Dragon"!!!**
I'm back on board! When
the crew got back on ship,
I crept on with them!
No one recognized me.

What bliss to eat real food again!
I never thought I'd enjoy hard
tack (that's pirate for biscuits)
so much, even if they are
crawling with maggots!

## 28 June

Captain Blackbeard spotted me today, but he ROARED with laughter at my cheek in getting back on board! He put me on lookout duty. Towards noon I spotted a Spanish merchant ship.

Ship ahoy!

At once, we took down our Jolly Roger and ran up a Spanish flag. Just to trick them, of course. We weren't really Spanish. Closer and closer we sailed.
Then we attacked.

We fought our way below decks.

What a sight met our eyes...

# Treasure beyond our wildest dreams!

In my pockets are enough gold coins to keep me in comfort for the rest of my life!

28 July: at home!
Very early this morning,
the "Dragon" slipped silently
into Seaside Harbour.

My job was to leap ashore with a rope
and tie up the ship. But I didn't see
that the rope was wrapped around my
ankle. Next thing I knew, I'd tripped
and was in the water - again!

I tried to swim to shore but my pockets were heavy with gold. I was being dragged down.

Suddenly I felt myself rising.
I was swimming strongly!

At last I reached the harbour steps
and clambered to the top. Ooh-aah!
Then I put my hands in my pockets.
Nothing! They were empty. All my
gold coins had fallen out.
Miserable maggots! All that trouble
and STILL I wasn't rich.

At home I read my new "Robbers' Weekly". An advertisement caught my eye.

Do you like working underground?
Are you good at keeping secrets?
Would you like to be very, very rich?

If the answer is yes, yes, yes,
apply now to:

Smugglers Inc.,
Sleepy Cove,
Well Hidden,
Cornwall,
SSH SSH


We can make your dreams
come true!

Sleepy Cove,
Well Hidden,
Cornwall,
SSH SSH

Dear Greasy Joe,
  I've joined Smugglers Inc.
Ooh-aah! Tonight, as soon as it
gets dark, we're going to — oops!
My lips are sealed.
        Hal

For James Andrew Ladislas
J. C.
For Ruth Whalley
P. D.

First published 2004 by Walker Books Ltd
87 Vauxhall Walk, London SE11 5HJ

2 4 6 8 10 9 7 5 3 1

Text © 2004 June Crebbin
Illustrations © 2004 Polly Dunbar

The right of June Crebbin and Polly Dunbar to be
identified as author and illustrator respectively of this
work has been asserted by them in accordance with
the Copyright, Designs and Patents Act 1988

This book has been typeset in Alpha-Normal, Calligraphic
and Calligraphic Antique

Handlettering by Polly Dunbar

Printed in China

British Library Cataloguing in Publication Data:
a catalogue record for this book
is available from the British Library

ISBN 0-7445-6595-2

www.walkerbooks.co.uk